Selected Translations of

Sagawa Chika's Poems

対訳

左川ちか選詩集

JN104662

Edited by Rina Kikuchi

Translated by Rina Kikuchi and Carol Hayes

菊地利奈＋キャロル・ヘイズ 訳

思潮社

本共訳プロジェクトは科研費15KK0049・15K01915、
2007年度・2009年度・2014年度・2015年度・2021年度
滋賀大学経済学部学術後援基金助成、2008年度・2013年
度・2019年度陵水学術後援会学術調査・研究助成、オー
ストラリア国立図書館2018 Asia Study Grant による研究
成果のひとつである。

This translation project was supported by KAKENHI Grant
15KK0049 and 15K01915, Shiga University Research Grant
in 2007, 2009, 2014 and 2015, Ryosui Research Grant in 2008,
2013 and 2019, and National Library of Australia 2018 Asia
Study Grant. The publication was made possible by Shiga
University Research Grant in 2021.

Selected Translations of Sagawa Chika's Poems

Edited by Kazuno Fujii
Photo by Hanayo
Designed by Sano Yuya

序　文

　左川ちかは、1911年に北海道に生まれ、28年に上京して文学活動を開始し、24歳の若さで亡くなるまでの7年間に、詩や散文を翻訳し、雑誌の編集にもかかわりながら、北園克衛（1902–78）や春山行夫（1902–94）らとともに、モダニズム運動の最先端をかけぬけた詩人である。

　左川は、おもに『詩と詩論』『MADAME BLANCHE』『椎の木』等の雑誌に発表、日本の現代詩が西洋のモダニズム、シュルレアリスム、ダダイズムといった新しい芸術運動に影響を受け大きく変容した1920年代から30年代に、さまざまな実験的手法を駆使し、新しい表現を模索した。

　1936年に左川が亡くなったとき、萩原朔太郎（1886–1942）、百田宗治（1893–1955）、西脇順三郎（1894–1982）、江間章子（1913–2005）らがその死を惜しんだ。その後も、富岡多惠子（1935–）、新井豊美（1935–2012）、小松瑛子（1929–2000）ら、次世代の女性詩人らによって語り継がれてきた。

　詩集としては、亡くなってすぐに伊藤整（1905–69）によって編集された『左川ちか詩集』（昭森社、1936年）をはじめ、『左川ちか全詩集』（森開社、1983年）、『左川ちか全詩集　新版』（森開社、2010年）、2022年には島田龍編『左川ちか全集』（書肆侃侃房）も刊行された。2015年には、中保佐和子が全訳した英訳詩集『The Collected Poems of Chika Sagawa』（Canarium Books）がアメリカで出版され、2016年に PEN America Literary Award を受賞。英訳がきっかけとなり、スペイン語、ポルトガル語、アラビア語など他言語へのひろがりをみせている。

左川ちかは川崎愛として、1911年に北海道余市に生まれた。父親は不詳。母チヨ、異父兄昇、異父妹キクと、余市に広大な土地を所有していた母方の祖父・長左衛門の敷地で暮らすが、左川誕生の頃にはすでに家は没落していた。幼少期に病弱であったこと、叔母のところへ数年預けられ母や昇と離れて暮らしたこと、兄妹三人それぞれの父親が違ううえに父親不在の複雑な家庭環境は、左川の人生に影を落とした。

　文学においても私生活でも重要な役割を担った人物として、7歳年上の川崎昇と、川崎の親友であり後に左川と恋人関係になる伊藤整が挙げられる。歌人でもあった川崎は左川にとって終生心の支えであり、よき理解者であった。1923年、左川は庁立小樽高等女学校（現・小樽桜陽高等学校）に進学。卒業の翌年、先に上京していた川崎と伊藤を追って川崎宅に身を寄せた。同郷の三人は、北海道の生活をそのまま東京に持ってきたかのように暮らし、文学活動にかかわってゆく。

　左川ちかの文学活動は、英語圏文学、特にモダニズム文学の翻訳から始まる。小樽高等女学校で英語教員の免許を取得した左川は、同じく英語を得意とした伊藤整とともに、英語作品の翻訳に取り組んでゆく。初めて紙面を飾った左川の作品は、モルナール・フェレンツ（1878–1952）の短編小説「Love and Deception」第1話の翻訳であり、自作の詩を発表する1年前の1929年4月、川崎と伊藤が手掛ける『文芸レビュー』に掲載された。1930年10月以降は、散文だけでなく英語詩の翻訳も発表するようになる。

　なかでも特筆すべきは、ジェイムズ・ジョイス（1882–1941）の詩集『Chamber Music』（1907）の全訳だ。三角関係と失恋をうたう

物語的連続性を持つ36篇の詩から成る本作品の和訳を、1931年1月から数篇ずつ1年以上かけて詩誌に発表。同じ時期にジョイスを翻訳していた西脇順三郎より早く初の日本語訳を完成させ、1932年8月、『室楽』（椎の木社）を出版した。

　左川は、西洋から入ってきたモダニズム思想に一読者として影響を受けるだけではなく、自身の翻訳行為を通して最先端の英語圏モダニズム文学に触れ、その手法を自身の創作にも活かしていった。1930年8月に、詩篇「昆虫」を川崎が編集する『VARIÉTÉS』に、「青い馬」を北園克衛らの『白紙』に掲載したあと、左川は次々と詩を発表していく。それはもはや西洋のモダニズムから影響を受けたというより、同時代の世界のモダニズム運動にその一員として参加したというにふさわしい。

　『室楽』訳において原作の韻を放棄し、散文詩形式で訳すなど、大胆で独創的なアプローチをとった左川にとって翻訳と創作の境界は曖昧だった。左川は、日本語と英語の境界を自由に行き来しながら、翻訳を含む創作活動を続けた。

　たとえば、『室楽』の最終連「彼らは勝ち誇り、長い緑の髪の毛をなびかせながら来る。彼らは海からやつて来る。そして海辺をわめき走る。私の心臓よ、そのやうに絶望して、もう睿智を失つたのか？　私の恋人よ、恋人よ、恋人よ、なぜあなたは私を独り残して去つたのか？」では、左川はあえて原詩の「my heart」を「我が心」（西脇訳）ではなく「私の心臓」と訳し、「絶望する心」という通常の日本語表現をディコンストラクトしている。左川訳の「私の心臓よ」という嘆きには、身体的な重みがあり、心臓を物理的につかまれたような苦しみがある。精神的苦痛だけではなく、そこから

流れ出る血という肉体的感覚と視覚的要素。ここに左川の独自性があらわれている。

　この「心臓」という言葉が持つ肉体的感覚と視覚的要素は、左川自身の詩にあらわれる「心臓」や「皮膚」、詩篇「死の髯」で流れる血にもつながっている。また、「髪の毛」「緑」「馬」「海」といった詩語も、左川の独特な詩世界を築き上げる重要なモチーフである。「なぜあなたは私を独り残して去つたのか？」という悲痛な叫びも、詩篇「緑」の最終行「私は人に捨てられた」や、「海の天使」と「海の捨子」の最終行「私は海へ捨てられた」といった表現につながり、さらには、詩篇「海の天使」の「大声をだし　訴へようと」するがその声は決して誰にも届かない叫びにつながっていく。

　生まれながらのモダニストと北園克衛が評した、左川の型にはまらない自由な精神と発想は、彼女のジェンダーとルーツに深く関係している。左川は、女性であり、かつ、北海道出身者であったことから、「大和文化」を軸として発展した「日本文学」の世界からはみ出した存在であり、当時の「詩壇」に属しようがなかった。左川は、二重の意味で周縁化された詩人だった。

　伊藤整が「（文壇の）主流」からはみ出しているというコンプレックスを生涯抱いたのに対し、左川はそのような苦しみにとらわれることはなかった。左川の関心は「文壇」に認められることではなく、つねに芸術表現とその手法に向けられていた。伊藤同様、左川にとっての「春」は、梅や桜や鶯ではなく、リンゴの花とカッコウの鳴き声であったが、左川はそれら非大和的なる要素を積極的に受け入れ、西洋モダニズムと融合させ、独自の詩世界を築き上げた。伊藤と左川は、ヨシキリやカッコウ、雪、荒波の石狩の海、落葉松

の林など故郷のモチーフを共有し、ともに英語圏モダニズム文学の翻訳行為を自らの表現手法として発展させながら、伊藤が詩作をあきらめ小説の道に進んだのに対し、左川はこれらのモチーフを積極的に取り入れてモダニズム詩の担い手となった。

　左川は本来、比較文学の視点からも女性詩研究の視点からも重要な位置をしめてしかるべきにもかかわらず、その研究は、まだ緒についたばかりである。研究が遅れたことにはさまざまな要因が考えられるが、ひとつには、藤本寿彦が指摘するように、左川が女性であるために、「男性詩人に偏りすぎた前衛詩研究」界で長年研究対象になりにくかったことが考えられる。たとえば、ジョイスの『Chamber Music』の訳を最初に完成させ出版したのは左川であるのに、西脇訳が最初であるかのように語られてきたことにも、その傾向が垣間見える。
　さらに、左川の作品は、当時の女流詩人たちの特質を備えていなかったがために、フェミニズム文学研究からも抜け落ちてしまった。水田宗子、エリス俊子、鳥居万由実らによって、左川が母という産む性や妻として与えられた家庭内の「女性の役割」にとらわれない女性を描いたことが指摘されているが、このように女性学の視点から左川が論じられるようになるには21世紀を待たなければならなかった。

　詩法においても、左川詩は1930年代前後の女性作家や詩人の特徴のひとつである「私語り」の要素を備えていない。当時の女性たちは、男性作品からの「独自性」を築くために、平塚らいてう（1886–1971）が「告白的感想文」とも呼んだ生活体験に基づいた創

作法をこぞって利用したが、左川の詩はこのような自伝的で主観的な手法とは無縁だ。

　左川は、当時の女性詩人としては珍しいほどに女性文芸誌やフェミニズム運動とかかわりがなかった。左川は雑誌の編集にもかかわったが、その文学的関心はフェミニズムではなく、もっぱら国内外の前衛詩運動にむけられていた。左川の詩法へのこだわりは、「こんな注意をして、効果を考へて構成された詩がいくつあるだらうか。たいていはその場の一寸した思ひ付きで詩を書いてゐるにすぎないのではないかしら。それでよい場合もある。併しそんな詩は既に滅びてゐる。平盤な生命の短いものであつた」（「魚の眼であつたならば」）にも端的にあらわれている。

　批評眼を備えた左川が目指したものは「滅びない詩」であった。鳥居万由実が指摘するように、モダニズムの手法は「理論的に主体的な「人間」の消去を目指して」いることから、主観的な「私」の人生や生活から、詩を切り離すことを可能にした。左川は翻訳という行為を通して身につけたモダニズム手法を自作に取り入れることによって、「私」という個人を超えた「私」を描くことに成功したといえる。

　村野四郎（1901–75）は、戦前の女性詩人に共通する特徴として「輪郭のぼやけた主観的成熟」を挙げて批判し、対して戦後の女性詩人らが「極力主観的膨張を抑えて、おのれの内面を客観視するだけの知的な詩的教養をも」ち、戦前の女性詩人らがなしえなかった新鮮な独自の詩世界を確立したことを讃えたが、左川は、1930年代前半の段階ですでに告白的で主観的な「私」を超えた「私」を描いていたといえる。このような左川詩の神髄を西脇順三郎は「非常

に女性でありながら理知的に透明な基本のある思考」と呼んだ。

　当時、相反すると考えられていた「女性性」と「理知的な思考」の融合が左川詩にはある。左川の詩には、母や妻という女性に与えられた社会的役割に縛られない「私」であり、かつ、自伝的な個人の物語に集約されない「私」、しかし記号としてではなく、存在感と肉体的重みを感じる「私」がある。

　左川ちかの詩に出会ったのは、2006年3月、アイルランド文学を翻訳していた伊藤整の資料調査でむかった小樽だった。彼女の言葉はまさに私の心臓をわしづかみにした。2011年から共訳者のキャロル・ヘイズとふたり、左川の言葉に溺れ窒息しそうになりながら、オーストラリア国立大学のキャンパスで共訳を開始。私たちは日本とオーストラリアを行き来しながら、顔をつき合わせて共訳作業を続けた。

　英語と日本語というふたつの言語を行き来しながら、新しい詩法を模索し詩の創作に挑んだ左川ちか。その左川の作品を、日英バイリンガル文学研究者の私たちも、言語の境界線を行きつ戻りつ、読み味わいわかちあい、共訳した。これらの作品を日英対訳で出版することによって、二言語ならではの共鳴と重奏性を体現できるのではないかと考え、この対訳詩集のアイデアが生まれた。

　この間、小野夕馥、中保佐和子、島田龍の各氏に資料や情報を提供いただいたほか、多くの方からたくさんの励ましと助言をいただいた。北海道では、市立小樽文学館、北海道立文学館をはじめ、左川が通った小樽桜陽高等学校、伊藤整が通った中学校に属する潮陵記念館と小樽商科大学の付属図書館及び歴史編纂室で資料を閲覧さ

せていただくことができた。伊藤もその創立に尽力した日本近代文学館、2018年アジア研究員となったオーストラリア国立図書館にもお世話になった。

　たくさんの出会いが、「左川ちか生誕110周年記念会」の開催につながった（2021年2月14日、滋賀大学）。本公開ワークショップでは、エリス俊子、中保佐和子両氏をゲストスピーカーに、坪井秀人、佐藤亨、カニエ・ナハ、奥間埜乃、藤井一乃氏を迎え、詩人、翻訳者、編集者、研究者等、さまざまな立場から左川詩の魅力を語り合った。

　また、本書の刊行にあたり、水田宗子、エリス俊子、松尾真由美の三氏から推薦の言葉をいただくことができた。思潮社の担当編集者である藤井さんは、えんえんと左川詩に対する情熱と愛を語りながら、なかなか論がまとまらない私に、いつでも辛抱強く耳を傾け、挫折しそうになるたびに叱咤激励してくださった。藤井さんがいなければ、この本は今も私の夢の中にしか存在しなかった。心からの感謝を捧げたい。

北アイルランド出身で1995年にノーベル文学賞を受賞した詩人シェイマス・ヒーニー（1939–2013）が説き続けた、「周縁であると同時に中心であること」。私は左川の詩を読むたびにそのことを思い出す。世界は今、周縁からの声を認め、周縁を中心に迎えようとしている。中心にあるものが定める基準である「主流」に認められることや、「主流」であることを求める必要がない世界へと、私たちは動き出している。

　そんな今だからこそ、周縁が中心であり、言語も文化も性も「私」という存在さえも流動的な左川が繰り広げる詩世界を「魚の眼」で見つめ楽しんでいただければ、それにまさる喜びはない。そこでは誰もが、何重層にもわたる仮面や殻に隠れる「私」となる。そして、「私」であり「私」ではない「私」は、「あなた」にもなる。

　最後になったが、2022年10月にがんで亡くなったキャロル・ヘイズに、この世とあの世の境を超え、この本を届けたい。

晩夏のキャンベラにて
菊地利奈

Sagawa Chika (1911–1936) was a pioneer Japanese woman poet, who was long 'hidden' but 'rediscovered' around the centenary year of her birth. At a time of dynamic poetic development influenced and inspired by the principles of modernism, surrealism and dadaism from Europe in 1920s and 30s, she created not only experimental but artistically successful poetry both in terms of thematic content and style. Her poems powerfully capture the complexities of women's lives in modernity and are still relevant or even more reflective in the 21st century.

Sagawa made an important contribution to the developmental stage of the modernism movement, along with Kitasono Katsue (1902–78) and Haruyama Yukio (1902–94), who later came to be acknowledged as the fathers of Japanese poetic modernism. A number of her contemporaries, including Hagiwara Sakutaro (1886–1942), Momota Soji (1893–1955), Nishiwaki Junzaburo (1894–1982) and Ema Shoko (1913–2005), mourned the loss of this prominent poetic talent when Sagawa died of stomach cancer at the age of 24. Her poetry has inspired women poets of later generations such as Tomioka Taeko (b.1935), Komatsu Eiko (1929–2000), Shiraishi Kazuko (b.1931), Arai Toyomi (1935–2012), Mizuta Noriko (b.1937) and Sawako Nakayasu (b.1975).

Despite the recognition Sagawa received from fellow poets, academic discourse failed to take up her work. Sagawa has been marginalised both by literary critics and by feminists. One of the reasons is the lack of literary interest and attention given to Japanese women's poetry written prior to the Second World War. Though women's poetry has been more widely studied since the 1980s, the main critical focus has been on post-WWII women poets. Another reason is that Sagawa rarely engaged with 'womanly' themes such as female empowerment, motherhood, childrearing and other domestic works. As a result, she became largely left out of feminist studies, which should by rights have included Sagawa along with other women writers of her time.

I 'discovered' Sagawa's poetry in 2006, when I was researching translations of Irish literature by Japanese modernist writers. Sagawa translated many modernist writings from English to Japanese, including poems, short stories and essays by James Joyce (1882–1941), Virginia Woolf (1882–1941) and Aldous Huxley (1894–1963). When I encountered Sagawa's own poetry, I found it different from other Japanese women's poetry of the time. Her powerful imagery and contemporariness struck me. Her creative mind was clearly influenced by the act of translation. Sagawa's writings do not mimic the works of these writers she translated. Rather, I argue she was a fully contributing member of the world modernism movement. The 24 poems selected for this book demonstrate her poetic experimentation both thematically and stylistically and the freshness and uniqueness of her metaphors and language-usage in relation to Western modernist writings, which she both read and translated. For details about the individual poems, see the 'Notes on Translation'.

Sagawa Chika, whose birth name was Kawasaki Chika, was born in Yoichi, Hokkaido, Japan, in 1911, into a wealthy family, which was in decline after her maternal grandfather, Chozaemon's death prior to her birth. Her father is unknown, and she grew up with her mother, Chiyo, her elder half-brother, Noboru, and her younger half-sister, Kiku in Chozaemon's estate in Yoichi. Despite suffering from recurrent illnesses throughout her childhood, she obtained a license to teach English and graduated from Otaru Municipal Women's High School in 1928.

Soon after her graduation, she moved to Tokyo and there her literary career began. Sagawa gravitated to Tokyo in the footsteps of two men, who played an important role in her literary and private life. One was Kawasaki Noboru (1904–87), her half-brother who was a tanka poet. The other was Ito Sei (1905–69), who later became a well-known novelist, translator and literary critic. Kawasaki was always supportive and understanding of his sister's literary career. One of Sagawa's first extant poems, 'THE BEETLE', was published in *VARIÉTÉS*, the literary journal Kawasaki was editing at the time.

Ito also grew up in Otaru. He was a life-long best friend of Kawasaki and became Sagawa's lover. Ito's sudden marriage to another woman in September 1930 affected Sagawa deeply. However, the two continued to closely work together even after Ito's marriage. Ito was an important figure in Japanese literary history as a translator who introduced 'new writings' from the West. He distributed texts to Sagawa and other fellow writers and poets to translate. While Ito co-translated Joyce's *Ulysses* with his scholar friends, Sagawa translated Joyce's *Chamber Music*, often with Ito beside her. It was Sagawa, who published the first completed Japanese translation of *Chamber Music* in 1932, not Nishiwaki Junzaburo, as often claimed. Translating Joyce had a significant impact on her own poems and we can see that particularly in her unique use of language.

During her short literary career, spanning 1929 to 1936, Sagawa published nearly 90 poems, about 15 essays, and many translations from English. The first collection of her poems, *Selected Poems of Sagawa Chika* was edited anonymously by Ito Sei and published in 1936, eleven months after her death. Three different versions of *Collected Poems of Sagawa Chika* were published in 1983, 2010 and 2017. However, they were all limited editions and they quickly became expensive rare books. This was one of the factors that resulted in this talented poet remaining 'hidden'. To make Sagawa's works accessible and widely available, the new *Complete Works of Sagawa Chika* edited and annotated by Ryu Shimada was published in 2022.

In 2015, *The Collected Poems of Chika Sagawa* edited and translated by Sawako Nakayasu was published. Sagawa's poems have also been translated in Spanish, Portuguese, Arabic, and other languages. We have chosen to publish this book bilingually to present echoes of the creative mind moving between two languages, for we believe Sagawa wrote these poems by going back and forth between English and Japanese, and also between translating poetry and writing poetry of her own.

I would like to acknowledge Toshiko Ellis, Mizuta Noriko, Matsuo Mayumi, Sawako Nakayasu, Ryu Shimada, Yu Ono, Toru Sato and

Hideto Tsuboi for their advice and information on Sagawa Chika. I thank Molly Lynde-Recchia and Penelope Layland for their advice on our English translations. I am most grateful to Kazuno Fujii, editor of Shicho-sha publisher, for her support and encouragement in the past two years. This book is dedicated to my long-term co-translator,

Carol Hayes, who started to co-translate these poems with me in 2011 at the Australian National University and passed away in October 2022.

February 2023, Canberra

Rina Kikuchi

CONTENTS

写真————花代
デザイン——佐野裕哉

Selected Translations of

Sagawa Chika's Poems

昆虫

昆虫が電流のやうな速度で繁殖した。
地殻の腫物をなめつくした。

美麗な衣裳を裏返して、都会の夜は女のやうに眠つた。

私はいま殻を乾す。
鱗のやうな皮膚は金属のやうに冷たいのである。

顔半面を塗りつぶしたこの秘密をたれもしつてはゐない
のだ。

夜は、盗まれた表情を自由に廻転さす痣のある女を有頂
天にする。

THE BEETLE

Beetles multiplied with the speed of an electric current.
Licking clean the swellings of the outer-shell of the earth.

With her outer garments turned inside out, the city-night slept
like a woman.

It is now that I dry out my shell.
My scaly skin is cold like metal.

There is no one who knows the secret of this painted-out
half-face.

The night delights the scar-faced woman, who is free to circulate
each stolen expression.

青い馬

馬は山をかけ下りて発狂した。その日から彼女は青い食物をたべる。夏は女達の目や袖を青く染めると街の広場で楽しく廻転する。

テラスの客等はあんなにシガレットを吸ふのでブリキのやうな空は貴婦人の頭髪の輪を落書きしてゐる。悲しい記憶は手巾のやうに捨てようと思ふ。恋と悔恨とエナメルの靴を忘れることが出来たら！

私は二階から飛び降りずに済んだのだ。

海が天にあがる。

BLUE HORSE

The horse went mad galloping down the hill. That was the day she started eating blue food. Summer dyes the women's eyes and sleeves blue and then joyfully spins around and around the town plaza.

The customers in the open-air cafés smoke so many cigarettes that the tin-plate sky scribbles ringlets in the fine ladies' hair. I'm thinking of throwing my sad memories away, just like discarding a handkerchief. If only I could forget my romance, my remorse and my patent-leather shoes!

I didn't have to jump from the second floor.

The sea rises to the heavens.

死の髯

料理人が青空を握る。四本の指跡がついて、
──次第に鶏が血をながす。ここでも太陽はつぶれてゐ
る。
たづねてくる青服の空の看守。
日光が駆け脚でゆくのを聞く。
彼らは生命よりながい夢を牢獄の中で守つてゐる。
刺繍の裏のやうな外の世界に触れるために一匹の蛾とな
つて窓に突きあたる。
死の長い巻鬚が一日だけしめつけるのをやめるならば私
らは奇蹟の上で跳びあがる。

死は私の殻を脱ぐ。

DEATH'S BEARD

The cook grasps the blue sky. Leaving four fingerprints
— slowly, he bleeds the chicken. Here too, the sun has been
crushed.

The sky guard dressed in blue comes to visit.

And listens to the sunlight's running feet.

In jail, they protect their dreams, longer than a single life.

Turning into a single moth, I fly up to the window trying to
touch the outer world — a world like the underside of a piece
of embroidery.

If death's long curling beard would stop strangling us for just
one day, we could jump up onto this miracle.

Death peels off my shell.

幻の家

料理人が青空を握る。四本の指あとがついて、次第に鶏が血をながす。ここでも太陽はつぶれてゐる。

たづねてくる空の看守。日光が駆け出すのを見る。

たれも住んでないからつぽの白い家。

人々の長い夢はこの家のまはりを幾重にもとりまいては花弁のやうに衰へてゐた。

死が徐ろに私の指にすがりつく。夜の殻を一枚づつとつてゐる。

この家は遠い世界の遠い思ひ出へと華麗な道が続いてゐる。

The cook grasps the blue sky. Leaving four fingerprints, slowly, he bleeds the chicken. Here too, the sun has been crushed.

The sky guard comes to visit. And sees the sunlight's running feet. The empty white house where nobody lives.

Everyone's long dreams have wrapped themselves around this house layer upon layer and then decayed like petals of flowers.

With slow deliberation, death clings to my fingers. Peeling away the night's shell one layer at a time.

It is from this house that a beautiful road leads towards the distant memories of the distant world.

白と黒

白い箭が走る。夜の鳥が射おとされ、私の瞳孔へ飛びこむ。
たえまなく無花果の眠りをさまたげる。
沈黙は部屋の中に止ることを好む。
彼らは燭台の影、拗られたプリムラの鉢、桃花心木の椅
子であつた。時と焰が絡みあつて、窓の周囲を滑走して
ゐるのを私はみまもつてゐる。
おお、けふも雨の中を顔の黒い男がやつて来て、
私の心の花苑をたたき乱して逃げる。
長靴をはいて来る雨よ、
夜どほし地上を踏み荒してゆくのか。

BLACK AND WHITE

The white arrow flies true. Shot, fallen, the night bird dives deep into my pupil.

Endlessly disrupting the sleep of the fig.

Silence prefers to remain motionless in the room.

They are the shadows of the candelabras; the pots of stripped primroses; the mahogany chairs. I watch over them as time and flame tangle together, sliding up and around the windowsills.

Oh, the man with a black face comes in through the rain again today violating the flower garden of my heart, he runs off.

Rain! Stomping in with your high boots,

will you be trampling the ground all night?

夢

真昼の裸の光の中でのみ崩壊する現実。すべての梓は白い骨である。透明な窓に脊を向けて彼女は説明することが出来ない。只、彼女の指輪は幾度もその反射を繰り返した。華麗なステンドグラス。虚飾された時間。またそれ等は家を迂回して賑やかな道をえらぶだらう。汗ばんだ暗い葉。その上の風は跛で動けない。闇の幻影を拒否しながら、私は知る。人々の不信なことを。外では塩辛い空気が魂をまきあげてゐる。

A DREAM

Reality that disintegrates just in the naked midday light. The ash trees all white bone. Her back to the transparent window, she cannot explain. Only her ring repeats reflection on reflection. Ornate stained glass. Time is ostentatious. They'll probably choose the bustling path, bypassing this house. Dark leaves, moist with sweat. Above them, the crippled wind cannot move. Rejecting such visions of darkness, I become aware — of human unfaithfulness. Outside the salty air whirls the souls up.

白く

芝生のうへを焔のやうにゆれ
アミシストの釖がきらめき
あなたはゆつくりと降りてくる
山鳩は失つた声に耳を傾ける。
梢をすぎる日ざしのあみ目。
緑のテラスと乾いた花卉。
私は時計をまくことをおもひだす。

FADING

glimmering like a flame on the grass

amethyst buttons glittering

slowly you come down this way

A mountain dove listens for the lost voice.

Rays of sunlight slant through the branches.

A green terrace and thirsty petals.

I remind myself to wind my watch.

緑

朝のバルコンから　波のやうにおしよせ

そこらぢゆうあふれてしまふ

私は山のみちで溺れさうになり

息がつまつて　いく度もまへのめりになるのを支へる

視力のなかの街は夢がまはるやうに開いたり閉ぢたりする

それらをめぐつて彼らはおそろしい勢で崩れかかる

私は人に捨てられた

GREEN

from the morning balcony   invading like waves

flooding over everywhere

I feel I am drowning on the mountain path

as each breath catches in my throat   I stop myself falling again

and again

the town captured in my vision opens and closes like a circling

dream

they come crashing in with a terrible force engulfing everything

I was abandoned

雲 の か た ち

銀色の波のアアチをおしあけ
行列の人々がとほる。

くだけた記憶が石と木と星の上に
かがやいてゐる。

皺だらけのカアテンが窓のそばで
集められそして引き裂かれる。

大理石の街がつくる放射光線の中を
ゆれてゆく一つの花環。

毎日、葉のやうな細い指先が
地図をかいてゐる。

CLOUD SHAPES

Opening an archway of silver waves
the line of people pushes through.

Shattered memories shine
above the rocks, trees and stars.

Near the window creased and wrinkled
curtains gather together and then pull apart.

A single wreath of flowers floats
through the beams of light radiating from the marble city.

Day after day, a fingertip leaf-slender
draws the map.

雲のやうに

果樹園を昆虫が緑色に貫き
葉裏をはひ　たへず繁殖してゐる
鼻孔から吐きだす粘液
それは青い霧である
時々　彼らは
音もなく羽搏きをして空へ消える
婦人達はただれた目付きで
未熟な実を拾つてゐる
空には無数の瘡痕がついてゐる
肘のやうにぶらさがつて
それから私は見る
果樹園がまんなかから裂けてしまふのを
そこから雲のやうにもえてゐる地肌が現はれる

LIKE CLOUDS

the line of beetles passes greenly through the orchard

crawling along the underside of the leaves   they multiply over
and over

disgorging mucus from their nostrils

it becomes the blue mist

from time to time   they

disappear into the sky soundlessly flapping their wings

women with inflamed eyes

gather up the unripe fruit

the sky has myriad scars

hanging loose like elbows

and then, I watch

the orchard splits right down the middle

and from that crack, the bare ground, burning like clouds,

appears

毎年土をかぶらせてね

ものうげに跫音もたてず
いけがきの忍冬にすがりつき
道ばたにうづくまつてしまふ
おいぼれの冬よ
おまへの頭髪はかわいて
その上をあるいた人も
それらの人の思ひ出も死んでしまつた。

YOU'LL PUT THE SOIL OVER EVERY YEAR, WON'T YOU?

walking, dispirited, without a sound

grasping the honeysuckle on the hedge

crouching down low on the road

Senile Old Winter!

Your hair is withered and

everyone who walked on it

and all memory of them is dead.

花咲ける大空に

それはすべての人の眼である。

白くひびく言葉ではないか。

私は帽子をぬいでそれ等をいれよう。

空と海が無数の花弁をかくしてゐるやうに。

やがていつの日か青い魚やばら色の小鳥が私の頭をつき
破る。

失つたものは再びかへつてこないだらう。

TO THE FLOWERING
WIDE-OPEN SKY

That is the eye of all mankind.

It's words, isn't it, whitely echoing.

I take off my hat to put them in.

Just as the sea and the sky are hiding the myriad petals.

Someday soon the blue fish and small rose-coloured birds will pierce my skull.

What is lost will never return, will it.

五月のリボン

窓の外で空気は大声で笑つた
その多彩な舌のかげで
葉が群になつて吹いてゐる
私は考へることが出来ない
其処にはたれかゐるのだらうか
暗闇に手をのばすと
ただ　風の長い髪の毛があつた

RIBBONS OF MAY

the air laughed loud outside my window

in the shadows of the multi-coloured faceted tongue

the leaves blow about in clumps

I am unable to understand

is there anyone out there?

I stretch out my hand into the darkness

it was only   the long hair of the wind

雪 線

　古ぼけ色褪せたタイムが熱い種子となつて空間に散乱する。無言の形態をとびこえ地上を横切る度に咲く花の血を吹きだしてゐる唇のうへでテクニックの粉飾を洗ひ落せ!!

　昨日の風を捨て約束にあふれた手を強く打ち振る枝は熱情と希望を無力な姿に変へる。その屍の絶えまない襲撃をうけて、歩調をうばはれる人のために残された思念の堆積。この乾き切つた砂洲を渡る旅人の胸の栄光はもはや失はれ、見知らぬ雪の破片が夜にとけこむ。何がいつまでも終局へと私を引摺つてゆくのか。

SNOW LINE

Faded with age, thyme turns hot seeds and scatters through the void. Wash off the adornments and fancy techniques!! Each time you fly over the wordless figures and traverse the land, wash them from the lips that blossom with flowers of blood.

The branches violently shake the hand that discarded the winds of yesterday, that hand which overflowed with the promise of engagements. The branches transform passion and hope into a powerless shape. A pile of thoughts is left behind for those who have had the rhythm of their steps stolen, under the relentless attack of that corpse. Honour within the hearts of the travellers crossing the desiccated sandbar is already lost and the strange splinters of snow blend into the darkness of the night. What drags me along forever and ever on towards the end?

プロムナアド

季節は手袋をはめかへ
舗道を埋める花びらの
薄れ日の
午後三時
白と黒とのスクリイン
瞳は雲に蔽はれて
約束もない日がくれる

P R O M E N A D E

seasons change their gloves

petals filling up the promenade

fading light

three o'clock in the afternoon

black and white screen

eyes covered by clouds

a day without a single engagement ends

会話

　——重いリズムの下積になつてゐた季節のために神の手はあげられるだらう。起伏する波の這ひ出して来る沿線は塩の花が咲いてゐる。すべてのものの生命の律動を渇望する古風な鍵盤はそのほこりだらけな指で太陽の熱した時間を待つてゐる。

　——夢は夢見る者にだけ残せ。草の間で陽炎はその緑色の触毛をなびかせ、毀れ易い影を守つてゐる。また、マドリガルの紫の煙は空をくもり硝子にする。

　——木の芽の破れる音がする。大きな歓喜の甘美なる果実。人の網膜を叩く歩調のながれ。

——真暗な墓石の下ですでに大地の一部となり喪失せる限りない色彩が現実と花苑を乱す時刻を知りたいのだ。

　——

　——不滅の深淵をころがりながら幾度も目覚めるものに閧声となり、その音が私を生み、その光が私を射る。この天の饗宴を迎へるべくホテルのロビイはサフランで埋められてゐる。

A DIALOGUE

— God's hand will be raised up to help the season apprenticed to the heavy rhythm. Salt flowers bloom along the railway line as it crawls out over the undulating waves. With dusty fingers, the old-fashioned keyboard waits for the time when the sun burns hot, longing for a rhythmic cadence.

— Leave dreams to the dreamers themselves. Amongst the grasses, heat-shimmer vibrates its green-coloured cilia-like hairs and protects its fragile reflection. Then purple madrigal smoke turns the sky to clouded glass.

— The sound of a leaf bud splitting open is heard. Utterly enchanting luscious fruit. The rhythm of passing steps taps the retinas of people.

— I want to know when the lost limitless colours, already part of the ground in the absolute darkness under the gravestones, disturb reality and the flowerbed.

—

— That sound, becoming the war cry for those who awaken over and over as they roll in the immortal abyss, gives me birth, and its light pierces me. The hotel lobby is buried in saffron flowers, ready to welcome this banquet of heaven.

魚の眼であつたならば

　つまらなくなつた時は絵を見る。其処では人間の心臓が色々の花弁のやうな形で、或は悲しい色をして黄や紫に変色して陳列されてゐるのを見ることが出来る。馬が眼鏡をかけて樹木のない真黒い山を駆け下りてゐる。私はまだ生きた心臓も死んだ皮膚も見たことがないので、とても愉快だ。なんて華やかな詩だ！　私は虫のやうな活字を乾いた一片の紙片の上に這はせる時のことばかりを考へてゐたから。美しい色が斑点となつて風や海の部分を埋めてゐる。画家の夢が顔料でいつぱいに染つて、まだ生々しく濡れてゐるのだ。馬鹿気た落書きなんだらうと思ひながら、あのずたずたに引き裂かれた内臓が輝いてゐるのを見ると、身顫ひがする位気持ちがよい。跳躍してゐるリズム、空気の波動性。この多彩な生物画が壁に貼りつけられて、眼の前で旋回してゐるのは一つの魅力である。

　画家は瞬間のイメエジを現実の空間に自由に具象化することの出来る線と色をもつてゐる。彼の魔術は凡てのありふれた観念を破壊することに成功した。太陽と精神内の光によつて細かに分析された映像を最も大胆に建設してゆく。時には人の考へたこともなかつたものに形を

与へてくれた。又、いつも見馴れて退屈してゐるものを
ぶちこわして新しい価値のレツテルを貼る。画家の仕事
と詩人のそれとは非常に似てゐると思ふ。その証拠に絵
を見るとくたびれる。色彩の、或はモチイフにおける構
図、陰影のもち来らす雰囲気、線が空間との接触点をき
める構図、こんな注意をして、効果を考へて構成された
詩がいくつあるだらうか。たいていはその場の一寸した
思ひ付きで詩を書いてゐるにすぎないのではないかしら。
それでよい場合もある。併しそんな詩は既に滅びてゐる。
平盤な生命の短いものであつた。

　私たちは一個のりんごを画く時、丸くて赤いといふ観
念を此の物質に与へてしまつてはいけないと思ふ。なぜ
ならばりんごといふ一つのサアクルに対して実にいいか
げんに定められた常識は絵画の場合に何等適用されるこ
との意味はない。誰かが丸くて赤いと云つたとしてもそ
れはほんのわづかな側面の反射であつて、その裏側が腐
つて青ぶくれてゐる時もあるし、切断面はぢくざくとし
てゐるかも知れない。りんごといふもののもつ包含性と
いふものをあらゆる視点から角度を違えて眺められるべ
きであらう。即ちもつと立体的な観察を物質にあたへる

ことは大切だと思ふ。詩の世界は現実に反射させた物質をもう一度思惟の領土に迄もどした角度から表現してゆくことかも知れない。

　私は今まで一つの平面の対角線の交点ばかりを見てゐた。その対角線に平行する空間を過ぎる線のことや対角線に垂線を下した場合などに気付かない時が多かつた。黒か白の他に黒でもない白でもないぼんやりとぼかしたやうな部分がこの空間をどんなに占めてゐるのだらう。そんな網の目のやうな複雑な部屋の窓を開けることはまたどんなに楽しいだらう。私は自分の力でこぢ開けなければと思ふ。

展覧会では完成した絵をいくつも見た。なる程うまい
かも知れない。併しそのやうな絵は面白くない。それは
結局一つの区域内の完成、運動の停止であつて、行き詰
つてゐることを語る以外の何物でもない。私はむしろ破
綻のあるものに魅力を感じた。その時の動揺は将来性を
示してゐるやうに思はれた。それから又随分映画の影響
を受けてゐる作品が多いと思つた。シルウエトや黒と白
の明暗の使ひわけなど。落ちぶれたゴツホや太陽の二つ
あるやうな絵もあつた。

　疲れて足が地面につかないやうな気がしたけれど外へ
出たら若い緑が目にしみた。

When things get boring I look at paintings. In these paintings, I can see human hearts shaped like myriad flower petals, displaying their sad colours, their transformations into yellows and purples. A horse, wearing glasses, races down a treeless black mountainside. These paintings are so fascinating because I've never yet seen a living heart or dead skin. Such splendid poetry! And here was I just thinking about making those wormlike letters crawl over a dry piece of paper. The beautiful colours reform into tiny specks and bury the wind and sea. Full of pigment, the colours of the painters' dreams are still wet and raw. Though dismissing these paintings as ridiculous scribbles, when I look at the gleaming of the intestines, ripped apart and torn to shreds, a shiver of pleasure runs through me. Their leaping rhythms, their undulating air. One of their charms is how these assorted paintings of living creatures, nailed to the walls, revolve in front of my eyes.

A painter uses lines and colours to freely transfigure an instantaneous image into the concrete in a real space. His magic is his success in destroying every mundane concept. Audaciously, he builds up each image, intricately analysed with the light of the sun and his own inner light. Sometimes, he manages to give shape to things for us, things that humans have never even thought about. He completely destroys all the things we are used to, we are bored with, and he creates categorised labels for new values. I think that the work of a painter and a poet are very similar. The proof is how worn out I feel when I look at paintings. The colours and motifs within a composition, the mood created by the shading, or the way the lines touch space within each image, I wonder how many poems are created by paying attention to these things, or by carefully thinking about their impact. I think in most cases people write poems on the spot just as the thoughts come to them. Sometimes it works. But such poems are already extinct. They are so common and short-lived.

When we depict a single apple, I don't think we should impose the concept of roundness and redness on this object. This is because the common concept of an 'apple' as a single 'circle' has been established without any real foundation and is absolutely meaningless when applied to a painting. Even if someone argued it was round and red, that would only reflect one tiny dimension;

sometimes the other side of the apple could be rotten and gangrenous blue, or sometimes it could be cut into zigzagged segments. We should look at the possible 'implications' of this thing called an 'apple' from many different perspectives and angles. Therefore I think it is important that we apply a three-dimensional observation to this physical object. Perhaps the world of poetry should express things that reflect reality from different angles that are drawn once again from the territory of deep thoughts.

Until now all I looked at was the intersection of the diagonals on a single flat surface. There were many times when I failed to notice the lines that projected through parallel planes sitting three-dimensionally beside those diagonals, or the verticals that can be drawn down onto those diagonals. Some areas are black and others white, but then some sections are neither black nor white, they seem to blur together and I find myself wondering, how much space is occupied by this clouded blur? And what a pleasure it would be to open the window, like the mesh of a net, in this so complex room. I feel I must wrench open the window with my own strength.

I also saw a number of completed paintings at the exhibition. Some may think these were good paintings. But such paintings are not interesting. This is because they only show completed perfection in one single area, all motion has stopped, they cannot tell us anything except that they have nothing more to tell us. But I was more attracted to something made up of disharmonious parts. I think that the sense of unease I felt at that moment somehow expresses potential for the future. I also thought that many of the paintings had been influenced by motion pictures. Such as the distinctive use of silhouettes or the balance of black and white. Some paintings looked like a Van Gogh in decline, or paintings that seemed to have two suns.

I was so tired my feet no longer seemed to even touch the ground, but when I went outside, the fresh greenery caught my eyes moving me deeply.

花

1

夢は切断された果実である
野原にはとび色の梨がころがつてゐる
パセリは皿の上に咲いてゐる
レグホンは時々指が六本に見える
卵をわると月が出る

2

林の間を蝸牛が這つてゐる
触角の上に空がある

3

今日は風の色が濃い
ピストンが塩辛い空気を破つて突進する
くつがへされた朝の下で雨は砂になる

FLOWERS

1

dreams are severed fruits
a red-brown pear lies fallen in the meadow
parsley is flowering on a plate
leghorns sometimes seem to have six claws
cracking an egg, the moon comes out

2

a snail crawls through the woods
on top of its feelers is the sky

3

today, the colour of the wind is deeper
the piston charges forward tearing apart the salty air
under the overturned morning, the rain turns to sand

午 後

花びらの如く降る。

重い重量にうたれて昆虫は木蔭をおりる。

牆壁に集まるもの、微風のうしろ、日射が波が響をころす。

骨骼が白い花をのせる。

思念に遮られて魚が断崖をのぼる。

Falling like flower petals.

Struck by a heavy weight, a beetle crawls down the tree shade.

Creatures gather at the fence, behind the breeze, the sunlight and the waves murder all sound.

Bone structure places a white flower.

Obstructed by thoughts, a fish climbs the cliff.

海 の 花 嫁

暗い樹海をうねうねになつてとほる風の音に目を覚ます
のでございます。
曇つた空のむかふで
　　　けふかへろ、けふかへろ、
と閑古鳥が啼くのでございます。
私はどこへ帰つて行つたらよいのでございませう。
昼のうしろへたどりつくためには、
すぐりといたどりの藪は深いのでございました。
林檎がうすれかけた記憶の中で
花盛りでございました。
そして見えない叫び声も。

防風林の湿つた径をかけぬけると、
すかんぽや野苺のある砂山にまゐるのでございます。

これらは宝石のやうに光つておいしうございます。

海は泡だつて、

レエスをひろげてゐるのでございませう。

短い列車は都会の方に向いてゐるのでございます。

悪い神様にうとまれながら

時間だけが波の穂にかさなりあひ、まばゆいのでござい
ます。

そこから私は誰れかの言葉を待ち、

現実へと押しあげる唄を聴くのでございます。

いまこそ人達はパラソルのやうに、

地上を蔽つてゐる樹木の饗宴の中へ入らうとしてゐるの
でございませう。

BRIDE OF THE SEA

It is I who awakens to the sound of the wind swirling through
the dark sea of trees.

Out in the distance of the cloud-filled sky

    kyō kaero kyō kaero— home today home today

It is the singing of the cuckoo.

I wonder where I should go home to.

Trying to reach that place behind the day

It is the gooseberry and knotweed in the undergrowth that
grow so thickly.

It is the apple blossoms

That are in full bloom within my fading memories.

So too are the crying voices I can no longer see.

When I run out on the path through the windbreak trees

It is the sand hills covered in wild strawberries and sour dock that I find myself in.

It is these fruits, glittering like jewels that are so delicious.

It is the sea foam

That seems spread out like fine lace.

It is the short train that leaves for the city.

Neglected by a wicked god

It is just my time that is so dazzling, rippling on the cresting

waves.

It is I, who wait there for someone's words,

And listen to the song that pushes me towards reality.

I wonder if, now more than ever, people, like parasols,

are trying to participate in the feast of the trees that conceal

the earth.

山脈

遠い峯は風のやうにゆらいでゐる
ふもとの果樹園は真白に開花してゐた
冬のままの山肌は
朝毎に絹を拡げたやうに美しい
私の瞳の中を音をたてて水が流れる
ありがたうございますと
私は見えないものに向つて拝みたい
誰れも聞いてはゐない　免しはしないのだ
山鳩が貰ひ泣きをしては
私の声を返してくれるのか
雪が消えて
谷間は石楠花や紅百合が咲き
緑の木蔭をつくるだらう
刺草の中にもおそい夏はひそんで
私たちの胸にどんなにか
華麗な焔が環を描く

MOUNTAIN RANGE

Mountain peaks sway as wind

The orchard at the foot of the range blossomed white

The mountain face still winter

So beautiful morning after morning like a silk cloth spread wide

Water flows a chattering rapid inside my eyes

'Thank you kindly'

I want to give prayerful thanks to something I cannot see

No one is listening   no one forgives

A mountain dove cries in empathy

I wonder if anyone will return my voice to me

As the snow melts

Rhododendrons and red lilies bloom in the valleys

Creating shady bowers

Late to arrive, summer stays hidden in the nettles

In our hearts, with such

Beauty, the flame draws a ring

海の天使

揺籃はごんごん鳴つてゐる
しぶきがまひあがり
羽毛を掻きむしつたやうだ
眠れるものの帰りを待つ
音楽が明るい時刻を知らせる
私は大声をだし訴へようとし
波はあとから消してしまふ

私は海へ捨てられた

ANGEL OF THE SEA

again and again the cradle crashes

sea spray dances high

like severed feathers

waiting for the one who sleeps

music heralds the coming of the bright hour

I scream aloud trying to make myself heard

the waves follow after and wash my cries away

I was abandoned into the sea

海 の 捨 子

揺籃はごんごん音を立ててゐる　真白いしぶきがまひあ
がり　霧のやうに向ふへ引いてゆく　私は胸の羽毛を掻
きむしり　その上を漂ふ　眠れるものからの帰りをまつ
遠くの音楽をきく　明るい陸は扇を開いたやうだ　私は
叫ばうとし　訴へようとし　波はあとから　消してしま
ふ

私は海に捨てられた

the cradle crashes and crashes again   pure white sea spray
dances high   disappearing into the distance like mist   I tear
the feathers from my breast   floating above them   listening
to the distant music   waiting for the return from the one who
sleeps   the bright land is like an open fan I try to cry out   trying to
make myself heard   the waves follow after   and wash my cries
away

I was abandoned in the sea

季節の夜

青葉若葉を積んだ軽便鉄道の

終列車が走る

季節の裏通りのやうにひつそりしてゐる

落葉松の林を抜けてキヤベツ畑へ

蝸牛のやうに這つてゆく

用のないものは早く降りて呉れ給へ

山の奥の染色工場まで六里

暗夜の道をぬらりと光つて

樹液がしたたる

A NIGHT OF THE SEASON

carrying piles of fresh and young leaves

the final train of the day runs along the narrow rail

as deserted as the back streets of the season

out of the larch forest into the cabbage plots

crawling along like a snail

'Step down to get out right now, those with nothing to do'

still fifteen miles to the dyeing factory deep in the mountains

the road on this dark night wet and gleaming

sap drips

翻訳について

　本書では、左川ちかの作品の一篇一篇を完全に独立したひとつの作品としてとらえ、各詩の特徴をいかすことを第一とした。そのため、訳詩のスタイルや表記法は、各訳詩によって異なっている。たとえば、行頭の大文字の使い方や句読点の使用法にみられるような詩形式が全体を通して一貫していないのは、そのためである。

　また、左川の詩が当時のモダニズム詩運動のまっただなかで書かれたものであり、詩の形式や表記に実験的なものが多いことに留意し、各詩の表現、表記、形式の特徴が、訳詩に反映するよう心掛けた。そのことは、左右のページを見比べていただければおわかりいただけると思う。たとえば、英訳詩中にみられる半角4字分の空白は、原詩の一字スペースに呼応している。また、「昆虫」をのぞき、すべての原詩は縦書で発表されているが、日英の比較がしやすいように本書ではすべて横書とした。

　左川の詩には改作改題された作品が数多くみられる。この事実を「定本が定まらない」とネガティブに受け止めるのではなく、左川が私たち読者に残してくれた多層な読み方の提示だと受け止め、それらのバリエーションを積極的に取り入れた。翻訳のうえでも、ヴァリアントを読み比べることが多くのヒントを与えてくれた。収録した「死の髯」と「幻の家」、「海の天使」と「海の捨子」は、ほぼ同じモチーフであり、同一作品とみなされることもあるが、本書では別作品として収録した。また、「魚の眼であつたならば」は、従来詩篇だとは考えられていないが、ジョイスの『Chamber Music』を散文詩に訳し、将来は小説を書きたいと抱負を語っていた左川の、詩と散文、批評と創作の境界を越えた実験的作品と考え、収録した。日本語のふたつのバリエーション、日英の言語のバリエーションを

読み比べ、重層的な読みの可能性を楽しんでもらいたい。

　左川の作品には日英言語の境、翻訳と詩作の境だけでなく、散文、詩、批評エッセイというジャンルの境界をやすやすと超える特徴がある。収録した24篇を読み比べることで、左川詩の境界を越える詩体験が読者の心のなかにも生まれることを願う。

　キャロル・ヘイズとの共訳作業は2011年から、伊藤整編の『左川ちか詩集』（昭森社、1936年）、『左川ちか全詩集』（森開社、1983年）、『左川ちか全詩集　新版』（森開社、2010年）を比較しながら、おもに昭森社版をもとにおこなった。「緑」「雲のやうに」「花」「海の花嫁」の4篇を除き、収録した詩篇は昭森社を底本としている。また、「魚の眼であつたならば」と「海の捨子」は昭森社版に収録されておらず、初出を底本とした。作品は原則として詩誌での初出年代順に並べている。今回の単行本化を機に、『左川ちか資料集成』（東都我刊我書房、2017年）、『左川ちか全集』（書肆侃侃房、2022年）にあたり、確認作業を進めた。

　本書は当初、筆者のアイルランド文学研究から派生した左川ちか研究の一環として、ヘイズと菊地の共訳プロジェクトとしてスタートした。筆者の左川研究は、滋賀大学経済学部学術後援基金助成「日本近代詩にみる英語詩の影響——伊藤整と左川ちかの詩を中心にして」等、2007年度以降複数の学内助成を得て、ポルトガル、オーストラリア等の国際学会における発表「The First Two Translations of *Chamber Music* in Japan」（2008年）、「The doubly marginalized poet: (re)assessing the poetry of Sagawa Chika」（2012年）、「Modernism and modanizumu: self-expression and stylistic challenges in the poetry of

Sagawa Chika」（2013 年）へと発展。2015 年度以降の科研費研究「1920–30 年代の日本の女性詩人・ジェンダー・主知的客観性に関する文学研究」及び科研国際共同研究加速基金研究につながった。

　私たちは、当時まだ知られざる存在であった左川詩への鍵となるような作品から翻訳を手掛けた。デビュー作の「昆虫」や「青い馬」、強烈な喪失感や絶望感など左川詩を特徴づける「緑」や「海の捨子」。さらに、左川詩への理解を深めるヴァリアント。左川の散文詩や小説への興味や詩法への探求が反映する「夢」や「雪線」。モダニズム的なイメージが組み合わさる「花」や「午後」に加え、物語風な「海の花嫁」や「山脈」。これらを翻訳することで、左川詩の豊かさを世界の読者に伝えたいと考えた。

　詩の翻訳にはさまざまな方法があるが、筆者は、詩の共訳をコラボレイティブ・アートとしてとらえている。私たちは、左川ちかと伊藤整がきっとそうしたように、ひとつのテキストを一緒に読み、議論し、相談し、意見を戦わせながら、妥協せず、対話を続け、着地点を探し合った。ひとりが日本語から英語に訳し、それを下敷き

にして他方が手を加えるというような分離作業はしていない。これらの英訳詩は対話の結果であり、それは左川の声を聞き取り、それを英語詩として読者に伝えようと奮闘した、私たちふたりの声の軌跡である。

　詩の翻訳に正解はない。翻訳のバリエーションで、一語、一行に何層もの意味があり、一篇の詩に、無数の読み方があることを示すことができる。また、原詩が読めない読者にとっては特に、複数の翻訳を読み比べることが、原詩への理解をより深める助けにもなる。原詩が日本語であるからこそ言語構造上可能になる多義性を、英訳詩からも読み取ってもらえるのではないかと考えている。

　日本語と英語、日本語によるヴァリアント、英訳のバリエーション、これらを流動し呼応させながら、読者のなかに新たなる詩世界が生まれること願ってやまない。左川の詩世界を完成させるのは、誰でもない、読者ひとりひとりなのだから。

　　　　　　　　　　　　　　　　　　　　　　　菊地利奈

Many of Sagawa's poems are experimental in forms and language, arising from her engagement with the modernism movement in 1920s and 30s in Japan. I have chosen 24 pieces that are representative of her poetic forms and challenges, and the experimental nature of Sagawa's work, which often sits on the borders between prose and poetry, poetry translation and poetic creation, and even critical essay and creative writing.

In these translations, Carol Hayes and I have approached each poem as an independent work and the format of each translation attempts to reflect the internal structure and cohesion of the original poem. To preserve the flavour of the original poems in the English translations, we have intentionally included some awkward phrasing and grammatical structures, which challenge English poetic conventions. We have also tried to capture the poetic forms and stylistic experimentations used by Sagawa, including her unique language usage, punctuation and grammatical reordering. If Sagawa has not used punctuation in the original, we have also chosen not to use punctuation in our translations, as long as the grammatical structure allows. The four-space large gap included in some lines indicates a similar space intentionally used in the original poem. Readers unfamiliar with Japanese script should note that Japanese sentences do not usually include any spaces.

All the poems presented here in Japanese script, except for 'THE BEETLE', were originally printed in vertical lines, which would have been read from right to left following Japanese convention, rather than the horizontal lines, read from left to right, that were introduced to Japanese printing from Western language conventions. We have followed the Western convention of horizontal line presentation for the Japanese originals to parallel the presentation of the English translations.

Since collections of her poetry have only been published after her death, there is no clear evidence of how Sagawa would have ordered her poems. We have chosen to follow the chronological order of the first publication date of each poem in poetic and literary journals. Some of her poems, such as 'DEATH'S BEARD' and 'THE ILLUSION OF A HOUSE', 'ANGEL OF THE SEA' and 'ABANDONED CHILD OF THE SEA', appear to be 'sister-poems' or variations of one poem. However, we believe these 'different versions' reflect Sagawa's experimentations and developing poetics and offer a deeper understanding of her poetry. Therefore, we have included them as separate poems. 'IF A FISH'S EYE' is not usually categorised as a poem but as a piece of prose. We argue this poetic essay is better categorised as a 'prose poem', and have thus chosen to include it in this book.

With regard to our translation process, we have chosen to jointly translate each of the poems, rather than assigning a lead translator to individual poems. First we read the Japanese original aloud. This allows us to better understand the rhythm of the work. Then we play with a number of possible translations, discussing tenses, grammatical particles and whether certain words are plural or singular. We each bring a different knowledge base to the table: one of us is an anglophone scholar of modern Japanese literature and the other a Japanese scholar of comparative literature with a focus on Ireland and Japan. We find this creates an interesting negotiation around the meaning in both languages.

In 2015, US-based poet and translator, Sawako Nakayasu published *The Collected Poems of Chika Sagawa* (Canarium Books). A reader can now compare and enjoy the different English-language translations of Sagawa's work, which we believe to uncover the multiple layers of the words, lines and poems in the original language. For instance, in Japanese, a simple word, タイム (ta-i-mu) in the poem 'SNOW LINE' could mean 'time' and 'thyme' at once. While we could not manage the same effect in our English translation, a reader can sense both meanings, we hope, by reading the two different translations of the same poem. Nakayasu says that her translation of Sagawa's poetry is 'one out of a myriad of the ways that each poem might be rendered in English'. So is ours. As the book of 100 different versions of one

17-syllable haiku poem by Basho, *One Hundred Frogs* by Hiroaki Sato, indicates, the more translations we have, the richer our experience of poetry in translation.

Except four poems, 'GREEN', 'LIKE CLOUDS', 'FLOWERS' and 'BRIDE OF THE SEA', we have incorporated in this volume poems previously published in *Poems of Sagawa Chika* (ed. Ito Sei, 1936). We have used the first periodical publication version of 'IF A FISH'S EYE' and 'ABANDONED CHILD OF THE SEA', because these poems were not included in the 1936 poetry collection.

We have followed the Japanese convention of family name followed by a given name for the names of Japanese poets. Some of the translations included here were published in *Transference* (Western Michigan University, Vol.2, 2014) and Shiga University Working Paper No.192 (2013) and No.221 (2015). The English 'Preface' and English 'Notes on Translation' are not a direct translation of the Japanese, as each aims to introduce the cultural and literary context of Sagawa's life and work to a different readership.

参考文献 | SELECTED BIBLIOGRAPHY

- ジェイムス・ジョイス／左川ちか訳『室楽』（椎の木社、1932 年）
- 『左川ちか詩集』（伊藤整編、昭森社、1936 年）
- 『左川ちか全詩集』（小野夕馥、川崎浩典、曾根博義編、森開社、1983 年）
- 『左川ちか全詩集　新版』（森開社、2010 年）
- 『左川ちか翻訳詩集』（森開社、2011 年）
- Nakayasu, Sawako, tr. *The Collected Poems of Chika Sagawa.* (Canarium Books, 2015)
- 『左川ちか資料集成』（東都我刊我書房、2017 年）
- 『左川ちか全集』（書肆侃侃房、2022 年）

　　　—

- ジェイムズ・ジョイス／西脇順三郎訳『ヂオイス詩集』（第一書房、1933 年）
- ジェイムズ・ジョイス／出口泰生訳『室内楽——ジョイス抒情詩集』（白鳳社、1972 年）
- 『伊藤整全集』全 24 巻（新潮社、1972–74 年）
- 村野四郎「解説」『日本の詩歌 27 現代詩集』（中央公論社、1976 年）
- 曾根博義『伝記 伊藤整——詩人の肖像』（六興出版、1977 年）
- Heaney, Seamus. *Preoccupations: Selected Prose, 1968-1978* (Faber & Faber, 1980)
- 富岡多惠子『さまざまなうた——詩人と詩』（文藝春秋、1979 年）
- 伊藤礼『伊藤整氏 奮闘の生涯』（講談社、1985 年）
- 江間章子『埋もれ詩の焰ら』（講談社、1985 年）
- 伊藤礼『伊藤整氏こいぶみ往来』（講談社、1987 年）
- 福田知子『微熱の花びら——林芙美子・尾崎翠・左川ちか』（蜘蛛出版社、1990 年）
- 江間章子『詩の宴——わが人生』（影書房、1995 年）
- Sato, Hiroaki. *One Hundred Frogs: From Renga to Haiku to English* (Weatherhill, 1995)
- 新井豊美『近代女性詩を読む』（思潮社、2000 年）
- 川西政明『昭和文学史』全 3 巻（講談社、2001 年）
- 『北園克衛全評論集』（沖積舎、2003 年）
- 藤富保男『評伝 北園克衛』（沖積舎、2003 年）

- 藤本寿彦『周縁としてのモダニズム──日本現代詩の底流』（双文社出版、2009 年）
- 川西政明『新・日本文壇史』第 5 巻（岩波書店、2011 年）
- 水田宗子『モダニズムと〈戦後女性詩〉の展開』（思潮社、2012 年）
- たかとう匡子『私の女性詩人ノート』（思潮社、2014 年）
- 鳥居万由実『「人間でないもの」とは誰か──戦争とモダニズムの詩学』（青土社、2022 年）

　　　──

- 菊地利奈「小樽高等商業高校における外国語教育──高商英語教育が伊藤整の文学活動に与えた影響」『滋賀大学経済学部研究年報』15 号（2008 年）
- 菊地利奈「『女人芸術』と生田花世──「私語り」とその文学的試み」『彦根論叢』393 号（2012 年）

　　　──

- 小松瑛子「黒い天鵞絨の天使──左川ちか小伝」『北方文芸──女流詩人特集号』5 巻 11 号（1972 年）
- 『詩と詩論 複製版』（教育出版センター、1979 年）
- 新川和江、吉原幸子編『現代詩ラ・メール』31 号、特集「資料・女性戦後詩」（書肆水族館、1991 年）
- 『江古田文学』63 号、特集「天才左川ちか」（日本大学藝術学部江古田文学会、2006 年）
- Ellis, Toshiko. 'Woman and the Body in Modern Japanese Poetry'. *Lectora*, 16 (2010).
- 和田博文監修『コレクション・都市モダニズム詩誌 第 13 巻 アルクイユクラブの構想』（ゆまに書房、2010 年）
- エリス俊子「左川ちかの声と身体──「女性詩」を超えて」『比較文学研究』106 号（2020 年）
- 島田龍「左川ちか年譜稿」『立命館大学人文科学研究所紀要』122 号（2020 年）
- Holca, Irina. 'Sawako Nakayasu Eats Sagawa Chika: Translation, Poetry, and (Post)Modernism', *Japanese Studies*, Vol.41 Issue 3 (2021)

菊地利奈│Rina Kikuchi

滋賀大学教授、キャンベラ大学客員准教授。近現代女性詩、現代アイルランド詩、比較文学。著書に日英対訳選詩集『Poet to Poet: Contemporary Women Poets from Japan』（ジェン・クロフォード共編、Recent Work Press、2017 年）、『Pleasant Troubles 喜ビ苦シミ翻ル詩：日豪対訳アンソロジー』（川口晴美監修、菊地利奈編訳、Recent Work Press、2018 年）他。

Rina Kikuchi is Professor of Literature at Shiga University, Japan, and Adjunct Associate Professor at the University of Canberra, Australia. She is currently working on a bilingual anthology of contemporary Japanese women poets and a research project on Japanese women's poetry of the Asia Pacific War. Her books include *Poet to Poet: Contemporary Women Poets from Japan* (Recent Work Press, 2017, co-edited with Jen Crawford) and *Pleasant Troubles* (Recent Work Press, 2018, co-edited with Harumi Kawaguchi).

キャロル・ヘイズ│Carol Hayes

オーストラリア国立大学教授（〜 2022 年）。日本近現代文学、日本文化研究。『現代詩手帖』2011 年 11 月号「特集・萩原朔太郎 2011」に寄稿。『Japan in Australia: Culture, Context and Connection』（Routledge、2019 年）共編、田中教子『闇と火と経』（澪標、2019 年）英訳部分担当。2022 年、旭日小綬章受章。2022 年 10 月逝去。

Carol Hayes was Professor of Japanese Language and Literature at the Australian National University. Her research interest was Japanese cultural production with a focus on modern Japanese literature and poetry and Japanese-language teaching. She was a co-editor of *Japan in Australia: Culture, Context and Connection* (Routledge, 2019). Her poetry translation includes a bilingual tanka poetry collection, Tanaka Noriko's *Darkness-Fire-Sutra* (Miotsukushi, 2019). She received The Order of the Rising Sun, Gold Rays with Rosette in 2022. She passed away in October 2022.

Selected Translations of Sagawa Chika's Poems

対訳 左川ちか 選詩集

著者
左川ちか

編者
菊地利奈

訳者
菊地利奈、キャロル・ヘイズ

発行所
株式会社 思潮社
162-0842　東京都新宿区市谷砂土原町 3-15
電話 03-5805-7501（営業）／ 03-3267-8141（編集）

印刷・製本
藤原印刷株式会社

発行日
2023 年 3 月 31 日

For the Bilingual Edition of
Sagawa Chika's Poems

Noriko Mizuta

The fierce sense of loneliness and the perception of an approaching end, which fill Sagawa Chika's poetic world, expressed through vivid, dry, violent, and discordant images, were doubtlessly nurtured by her early life in the severe natural environment of Hokkaido, a northern periphery of Japan. She lived there until the age of 17 in 1928, when she moved to Tokyo.

In Tokyo, her sense of the vulnerability of life was fortified by the turmoil of the metropolis in its era of rapid modernization, but she also found a radical and refined poetic expression through the sophistication of her language and through her contact with Western modernist poets and writers, including James Joyce and Virginia Woolf among others, whose works she translated. Sagawa shares with them the sense of being part of nature which exercises overwhelming power over the life and death of all creatures, in particular the power of oceans, rivers, and waves. Her radical, avant-garde use of language and images, as well as her disharmonious composition of poems, are the expression of her uneasiness and sense of threat, the experience of being a stranger living in a gendered, power-oriented society and world. Her writing was cut short by her death in 1936, a year before Japan launched its war in Asia. Although the body of her works is not large and she was not known to the public for a long time, she has had a tremendous influence on Japanese poets, particularly on women poets and writers, and she is considered today one of the most outstanding modernist poets of Japan.

『対訳 左川ちか選詩集』に寄せて

水田宗子

　北海道・小樽から東京へ出た左川ちかは、社会制度内への定着を拒み、近代文明の根無し草として、直接自然と対峙し、自然に翻弄され、救済される「いのち」の感性を表現した。左川の自然は、北国の厳しい冬の海、地割れする夏の果樹園だが、同時に、彼女が翻訳を手掛け、また敬愛したアイルランドのジエイムズ・ジョイスやヴァージニア・ウルフの自然を共有している。ジョイスの異邦人感覚、ウルフの性的はぐれもの意識と深く共鳴しあう感性。自然の不協和音と流れては炸裂するリズムに満ちた表現の具体性においても西欧モダニズムの詩人や作家と深い相似がある。

　そもそも西欧モダニズムはヨーロッパの周縁からの表現であったが、左川の詩は、近代文明の、精神への破壊力への恐怖と反逆の強烈な感性を表現の基盤としている点で、西欧モダニズムの詩と共有する世界を展開している。菊地利奈、キャロル・ヘイズによる翻訳は、左川をそうした西欧モダニズム表現に位置づけようとする視点が特徴である。強烈な視覚的イメージで書かれたテキスト表現の具体性をできる限り正確に示そうとする姿勢は信頼できる。

エリス俊子

　心臓にぐさりと刺さってくる左川ちかの詩。引きちぎられそうな身体をかろうじて支えながら、声にならない声を響かせて、24年の生涯を詩人として生き抜いた左川ちかの詩は、艶やかで、力強く、切なく、潔い。そこでは自然が獰猛に叫

び声をあげ、詩人は消え入りそうになりながら、足掻き、求め、愚痴一つこぼさずに、夢を見て、失われた夢をうたいつづける。

　妻にならず、母にならず、自身の女性性を高らかに掲げることもなく、モダニズム詩の世界で、一人、言葉と向き合い、言葉と格闘しながら、切り詰めた詩句を紡いでいった左川の声は、フェミニズムなどという表現が古めかしく思えるほど、一人立つ個としての婉美な斬新さがある。二十世紀英語詩の翻訳から出発した左川ちかが、同時代「世界」の詩人たちを心の友としていたことは、彼女の創造的な訳詩が自身の創作詩と連続的な関係にあることからも明らかだ。

　日英の対訳詩集で二言語を往還しながら、私たちは左川の詩世界の自由に少しばかり触れることができる。二言語の揺らぎに身を置いたとき、母語の壁に破れが入り、複言語世界の未然の領域が一瞬、目の前に切り拓かれる。この対訳詩集はそんな経験を与えてくれる。

松尾真由美

　北の地に生まれ早逝してしまった詩人・左川ちか。その作品群はいまも氷の透明感で光り輝き人々を惹きつける。硬質な文体が北海道生まれの私には氷をイメージさせるが、前衛的で感傷的ではなく、けれども、何かを摑もうとする所作としての儚さの現前化が胸をつく彼女の詩は、実に自然発生的に生まれたもののように思えている。湿っぽいものはすべて凍ってしまうという北海道の長い冬。氷点下の地は容易に死と近接し、乾いた空気はどこまでも広がって甘えを赦してはくれない。こうしたところでは己の涙や汗を主張することに違和があり、日本的抒情と乖離する感覚がある。そこに左川ちかの場合は外国文学が入ってくる。モダニズム的主体の身体はここで無理なく形成されただろう。虚弱な体質も表現者の孤独感を深める役割を果たしたのかもしれない。文学の師ともいえる兄や兄の友人の後押しがあっても主体の孤独は変わらない。むしろ、左川ちかの内にある冷たく寒い孤絶感が翻って各々の詩の熱度を象るのだ。

Ellis Toshiko

The silent cry of Sagawa Chika reaches you directly and captures your heart. Her poems, so elegant, upright, bold and powerful, were borne out of a frail body that struggled, with dignity, to resist giving in to its own fate. Sagawa lived the twenty-four years of her life dedicating her energy to writing poetry : yearning, lamenting, dreaming a lost dream that never was, carving her words with style so economical that we hear the voice of a bare soul, intensely loving, and loving more, unrequited. The nature around her is ominously roaring; the earth cracks, the green overflows, and the sun multiplies. And yet she adamantly stands, as woman, not wife or mother, but as a challenging modernist, a female more than a feminist, whose comrades were the early twentieth century modernists on the other side of the ocean or across the continent. Sagawa was a translator of English poetry, and she would be most excited, and I am sure thankful, to see her poems appearing in two languages in this small but charming collection.

Matsuo Mayumi

The work of Sagawa Chika shines and attracts us, even now, almost a century after her early death. Like myself she was born in the north of Japan, in Hokkaido, and her language reminds me of ice and crystals. I am deeply touched by her avant-garde and unsentimental spirit which struggles to grasp 'something' through poetry. Anything which has slightest moisture becomes frozen in our long winter. I know that reality in Hokkaido. Death is so close, it is all around us in our vast dry, below-zero land. We cannot sing of our tears and our sweat up here – our contribution to Japanese poetic tradition is a different one. For Sagawa, modernist literature from the West poured into her and filled her solitude as a poet. In her, and in her poetry, icy cold loneliness spreads and transforms into heat.